ARNAUD RYKNER

TRANSLATED BY
SUE BOSWELL

THIS IS A SNUGGLY BOOK

Original title: *Nur*
Original publisher: © Le Rouergue, 2007
Translation Copyright © 2025 by Sue Boswell
All rights reserved.

ISBN: 978-1-64525-174-3

ARNAUD RYKNER is a writer and academic. He has published nine novels, several of which have appeared in paperback including *Le Wagon* which won the Jean d'Heurs prize for historical fiction in 2011. He is a Professor and Director of Research at the Sorbonne Nouvelle in Paris, and has also authored a dozen essays and edited many collected works. As a theatrical producer he has notably put on the works of Nathalie Sarraute, Maurice Maeterlinck and Bernard-Marie Koltès. He is a Visiting Professor at Rutgers University and a Senior Research Fellow of the University of Durham.

SUE BOSWELL studied French Language and Literature at UCL and for a time taught French at Goldsmiths University of London. She then moved into university administration, specialising in external relations and communications. Later she became a translator for the Wiener Holocaust Library, and translated Arnaud Rykner's novel *Le Wagon* as *The Last Train* (Snuggly Books, 2020). Her other translations include Marcel Schwob's *The Assassins and other Stories*, Ilarie Voronca's *The Confession of a False Soul* and with her husband, Colin Boswell, Gustave Kahn's *The Mad King*, also for Snuggly Books.

SNUGGLY
BOOKS

You need a great deal of scepticism in order to be satisfied with what is. Those who love the absolute only reject what is through a passionate believe in what is perhaps not.

Louis Aragon

You know nothing. You understand nothing. You don't wish to understand. Never. You don't want to know how that could happen. You wanted that to happen. You had been waiting for ever. An impossible love. An unbearable love. A storybook love. Another love. And there it is, threatening everything, threatening to carry all away, your life, the lives of those you love, those whom you no longer know how to love, and whom you love nevertheless more than anything, more than anything but perhaps not more than that other love you dreamed of so much that it happened here, in this town.

You know nothing. You don't wish to know anything.

Nothing more.

Nothing.

Then you close your eyes. You see her. You see yourself in her. You are lost.

You met her of course during your travels, one of those business trips called a 'mission' by those who pay you, as if all the trips you made to bring back for them a little of that money that they don't know what to do with, as if all those trips depended upon a spirit of conquest combined with a spirit of service to the extent that they become indistinct – a journey far away, in a country previously unknown to you, a country which, to start with, frightened you, had almost made you abandon it on the day of departure, facing those kilometres to cross, facing the abandonment, if only temporary, of those you love.

Upon your arrival all the clichés had been there, for you, crowding around you, the Orient, foreignness, foreign people, everything that until now has put you off by the very banality of its being there already seen, already read, already lived by others, so many others of whom you did not want to be one, not for anything in the world. All that was an attraction classified before you by centuries of travels, thousands of travellers. A shoddy exoticism, you thought, which put you off in advance, which you fought against.

Everything, the smells, the colours, the commotion in the streets, the movements of the crowds, right up to the variety of faces, had surprised you, taken you by surprise despite, or because of, its very obviousness. You were caught, yes, well caught, by the absolute which suddenly overwhelmed you as you experienced the movements of those vertiginous bodies, with their scents of bazaars. Absolute, nothing more. Who can you explain that to? Who would understand? Who would be able to stifle their laughter, their mockery? The totality of an impossible love. The songs. The same old stories. The novels, too. The ridiculous Madame Bovary whose pitiful attire you so feared donning. And yet, despite everything, despite the grotesque nature of that mixture, of that, the absolute, the irreparable had appeared before you and you had welcomed it. And there you were, facing it alone, with no one behind you to give you shelter, with no family to protect you from it, with no friends to re-assure you. Alone, facing it. Alone, facing her. Surrounded by a solitude which had begun to close around you for ever. Around her. Around her, and you, alone. Just that.

It was no doubt at the bazaar that she appeared before you, or elsewhere, it's not important, but certainly amongst a crowd of other bodies where you hadn't noticed her in the commo-tion. It was only later, seeing the photos taken at that time, that you had realised that from that moment your eye, or your body stretched out behind your eye, dragging your gaze, had chosen her without warning, in the midst of the crowd. Several photos in fact focused on that woman whom you didn't yet know, whom you were even incapable of seeing whilst your very eye was seeing her and your camera was fixing her forever deep inside you. Later, on looking at those photos displayed next to each other, you would not understand how you had been unable to know at that moment that, already, her image would be the most powerful.

Perhaps the strangest thing about all that was that once her body had entered your story, once her presence had imposed itself onto your own life, nothing else really existed. As if a hitherto unsuspected door had opened, then closed behind you both, behind that exchange of your bodies, behind what circulates inside you. Then even if she carried inside herself all the seductiveness of the world from which you had dragged her, that world had faded away in her tracks and in that world which now you also were leaving behind you. A break in time, a gap in your bedroom wall, which seemed to have given access to another unknown room from which you would never be able to emerge, since you had never thought to turn around.

In that room which you entered freely, she undresses. First you look at her, for a long time, and she, standing before you, doesn't move. You say nothing, and she says nothing to the man who is looking at her. You feel her desire for you, but yet she gently resists that desire which threatens to overwhelm her but which she concentrates in your gaze. She is entirely in your gaze, in your gaze at her body that you don't yet want to touch, just gaze at, just love from afar.

Then, you touch her.

At first it's your hand on her skin for as long as you gazed at her, your hand motionless. Then your hand moves away, suspended for a moment in the air between you both.

In your turn, watching her, you slowly undress, torn between embarrassment and unbearable desire, whilst in her turn she watches you, watches the clothes clumsily dropping, one by one, stupidly ordinary, bewildering, now making a pile in front of you.

So as not to see that she's looking at you, so as not to look at her who in her own language is already trying to remember this moment so as never to be separated totally from it, so as not to see those eyes watching you, you close your own and lie slowly over her.

You are both breathing quietly, not panting, not moving, in that shared solitude. Perhaps it lasts for hours, perhaps days.

What is certain is that you are ashamed of the whiteness of your body, naked against her matt brown skin. Then she speaks. She tells you not to be ashamed. She says she likes that paleness. My husband is also white like you, his body white like yours. And yet he's from the same country as me. With us, men are often white. We kept all the sun for ourselves, some say. The women, brown, and the men white, white as the sheets we sleep on, white as arms keeping us for ever. As for me, I know that I am forever a prisoner of your body; I know that now I'm keeping your body for myself forever, that I belong to it, that I will never free myself from it. Never. Even after you leave. Especially after you leave. For you will leave, I know it, you know it. You will leave. It's the only thing we know we'll both have to live with for ever.

Perhaps that's not what she says, for her words are too clumsy; the words of your language are too foreign to her. But nevertheless that's what she says in her own words, with her body, with her caresses, with her silence. She speaks, and her voice speaks beyond the words she says, and her body speaks beyond the silence. She speaks, and you keep listening to her.

She speaks again about her husband. She says clearly that she is not ashamed of loving you, and yet she loves him, that other man with his pale skin and his smooth body, just as much. Her love for you detracts nothing from her love for him. She believes it, she is sure of it, perhaps she has never loved him as much as when she loves you, as making love with your body.

You say that you are like her. The same as her. Loving her is like loving again the one to whom you gave yourself long ago. Loving her is not complete treachery. It is continuing to love, loving in another way than calmly. Loving beyond the gloomy succession of days. Loving even more the one you love for ever. Few people will understand, no-one no doubt, and perhaps you yourself, later, won't understand. But that's how it is. You know it's like that, that it's the truth, that you're not cheating, you're not lying. You're sure of it. You have never been closer to yourself than at this moment. Closer to that truth which ties you to the one you love at a distance. How can you say it? There are no words. It is the words which lie. Not you. Not her.

Then you take her into your mouth. You hold her buttocks in your hands. She is entirely yours, breathed in, feeling your lips all over her, with her body stretched over yours, her hands on your ankles, her stretched out body ready to yield to that violence of your mouth. She cries out that it's unbelievable. She cries out whilst you laugh about it, incredulous. Before you even touched her you felt her ready to cry out with joy and pleasure, but now it's too much for her. You tell her not to do it, not to cry out, that it's not necessary, as if you believed that she was lying, that she was crying out like a bought woman paying with cries for the money she's been given. But it isn't that. Her cries have nothing to do with those of such women. As incredible as it seems to you, her cries do not lie. They simply express her pleasure, a pleasure so great one would like to die of it, pleasure quite simply. You are embarrassed by that pleasure, it's so strong, and at the same time there it is becoming yours. You share it, as much as one can share the other's pleasure, like their suffering, as much as one can share the solitude of pleasure. Her pleasure is your pleasure. Not through the idiotic pride of the male. It's something else reaching out to you through those cries. An unthinkable happiness, for making a body thus cry with joy is not permitted. You thought that that was not permitted, not possible. And yet that's how it is, you can see that that's how it is. You can hear it so loudly that you go to close the door. You laugh as you do it whilst she rests from having cried out so much. Then you go to join her and you lie down alongside her. She is saying nothing more. She's no longer crying out. You tell her, laughingly, that her own pleasure gives you so much pleasure that you could nearly believe that she's been sent to you for that, pleasure, and to get from you goodness knows what secret. Laughing, you call her a spy, knowing that apart from her you have scarcely any secrets. She says nothing.

One would believe she's now asleep. But she isn't sleeping. Her eyes are watching you.

Perhaps it was then that you gave her this name. This name that says too much, or not enough. This name, in another language which is neither hers nor yours. This name which you have chosen. *Nur*.

Nour in Arabic means *light*; but in German it means *only*. Only what? You don't know. Only her, only her body. Only her body, locked in this bedroom. Or you locked into her body. Nur. Only that. Everything. Nothing. Only now. And for how long.

For this story with her is leading you nowhere, only there, into this bedroom, this shared solitude, this solitude momentarily exchanged for cries. Solitude between her and you, between your body and hers, between the four walls where her body offered itself to you just a few days ago, less than a week. Just a week. Suspended between all the other days of your life.

Nur. She doesn't know you call her that. She thinks you don't know her name. In fact, you don't know it. All you know of her is her body and that syllable which you now call her by, softly. She closes her eyes then reopens them. Then closes them again whilst you murmur this name for her which you have given her and which she believes to be some word from your own language, one she doesn't know.

You kiss her.

You kiss the eyes beneath the closed lids.

Her own hand, blindly, suddenly runs over your body, as if your body's whiteness was making her move forward in the darkness of her closed lids, or as if she preferred to dream of meeting you inside her eyes. And you, like her, you would almost prefer not to believe this is true, to behave as if none of it was really happening; like her, you would prefer to believe that what you are seeing here is a digression, is not part of real life. To believe that it's a nocturnal life that you are both inventing for yourselves, in a dream you share by chance, as if you suddenly happened to be sharing the dream of another, to be entering it, and to be bringing her into your own, not a real dream of course, but a sort, yes, of a digression, again, of a halt to any other faculty than that of losing yourself in images. Images of another life, yet from now on your own, whether you wish it or not.

For now something you had searched for in vain for many years of theatre has descended upon you. To live the life of another: you're doing it. You're not playing a part, you're doing it. As if you lived inside another's body as if you had the body and the movements of someone whose life you previously read about and which now, really, you're living.

And now it's you who close your eyes, again, as to better feel this hand which is slipping over your skin, this hand which hesitates and which you would like to be bolder, but whose very hesitancy makes the contact so fragile and so violent. From the nape of your neck to your thighs, you feel it gliding in the silence of your bedroom. You keep your eyes closed.

Perhaps you're asleep.

Perhaps you're dreaming.

You're dreaming of that hand between your thighs, of that hand on your back, of that hand on your mouth, of those fingers between your lips, against your teeth, of her who speaks in a language you don't understand, an incredible language, of her who murmurs in a language as incredible as her cries, of her who is now singing softly whilst you dream of her, whilst you dream of her being close to you. Whilst this impossible love is happening.

Yes, it is perhaps during this dream that you decided never to leave her, never to go right away from her, and yet never to give yourself wholly over to her, but to keep between you the distance necessary to keep your love for her alive—so that it never ends, never dies. You've read that too. The story of a princess who was not from the East.

Happy are they who live the life of a book.

You dream of her now, here, and far away there, as if at the other side of the sea on which your dream cradled you long ago. You dream of her here and over there at the same time. You dream that it's forever. You dream. You dream it will be possible because of the distance between you both to keep her alive in your dream. You dream of keeping her without completely taking her. You dream of taking her again and again, making her cry in that incredible folly which she is now turning to song, of giving her again and again that suspension of all thought which with her cries she also gives to you. You dream of her with you, forever. You dream of her being only a cry and you dream that this cry could be your whole life, in the silence of all the future bedrooms to which your life will inevitably lead you. Until this very room where you will write her story, the story of her cries in that bedroom, that bedroom where you were perhaps already dreaming of writing this story which you perhaps have not lived, this story that perhaps you are only now dreaming. Who can say. This bedroom is the only real one, with that one where, in twenty or thirty years, scarcely more no doubt, if you die in a bed you'll have to pass on the other side of your life, this bedroom you enter each evening, a room with souvenirs, with nightmares, a room to write in, to light up in the dark, a room where the paper is the skin ripped from her, that skin you would sometimes like to tear, her skin that your hand caresses with your eyes closed, whilst your body rests against hers, here or there. You dream, perhaps, of raising a pyramid, a tomb where your body can rot, but where hers is fragrant with the scents of that Orient which you have never reached. A pyramid where from now on you could hide who you are, a pyramid where you will hide her forever, as in your most secret dreams, in your least accessible dreams, dreams in which no-one except her could ever join you, dreams where you yourself would not be able to find yourself, dreams despite yourself, a labyrinthine construct, with that death chamber at its core, where you rest at her side wither her cry of pleasure unending in the silence of that late morning.

How long do you stay like this, between two shores, between two cries? How long dreaming these parallel dreams stretching out to infinity? The city's quiet murmur comes back to you, as if the city had moved away whilst you took your pleasure. Her breathing lengthens. Calmed. Her body relaxes, sleep taking over.

You open the window.

You leave the bedroom.

You leave her asleep, in the slightly moist air coming up from the streets.

When you return she hasn't moved. Only her eyes are watching you again. You sit for a long moment with her eyes on you. In the mirror you see her watching you. She rises and joins you at the bedside. You're now side by side. You look straight ahead. You see yourself. The mirror reflects this brown and white picture, the disparate and splendid mix of your skins. The black marks of body hairs, hair and sexual parts. Human bodies, unadorned. A stunning spectacle.

That lasts a long time. You don't know how long, doing nothing, saying nothing, just looking in the mirror, wondering at the perfection of your difference. At your total proximity in that difference.

Finally she dresses, whilst you still watch her in the mirror. Then slowly she dresses you, even more slowly than you took off your own clothes. With as much desire as she watched you take them off, she puts them back on. You help her, clumsily; you slide into them, the shame greater at every moment, but the sweetness too. Your body has resumed its irritating banality.

Hers continues its splendour in the mirror, beneath the recovered clothing.

She ties up her hair, and the simple gesture stuns you more than all the rest.

Then, whilst she is doing her hair, you're thinking of only one thing: to understand how it will end, how you could continue living without thinking it has been a day, a week, perhaps a month if you stick with the 'mission' entrusted to you by your paymaster. And not knowing, not really understanding what's happening to you, what is growing inside you whilst you stand up, help her on with her coat, open the door for her, follow her, close the door, turn the key, and set off with her down the silent staircase. Once outside you let her move off without looking back, until the moment when you can again take her in your arms; you watch her disappear, already inaccessible, and you to decide not to go on thinking about it.

Setting off in the other direction you too mix with passers-by to cross the impossible city. You will walk.

What you like here is still and always understanding nothing. Taken into this crowd, this crowd looking like her. The 'language barrier'? But it's the language you understand that makes a barrier… How can you get closer to these unknowns than being amongst them and not understanding them. Not understanding will save you; you know it. Not speaking her language, she who doesn't really speak yours. Letting yourself be taken without understanding. Besides, who does? Who can ever understand those one crosses or those who face him? Not understanding, it is *not lying to yourself*, not lying. You're not lying to her. You're no longer even lying to yourself. In this crowd, only linked to you via your body, at last you are yourself, wordless, without that screen behind which you usually hide unwittingly. You're walking in full daylight, the sounds of the street with you, like so much encouragement not to stop again, to continue straight ahead, to leave for ever all business of words, signs, codes supposed to protect you. You're walking, lit by the street, lit by her body which gives you back yourself, no mask, no lies, and no words. She's the one who guides you, in her absence, whilst you imagine her beside that other man she loves. And the city is opening up to you.

Her city, however, is not a city like others. History is more present there than elsewhere, grasping you and making you look away. Ancient history and modern history, because, as they say, the history of the world plays out here, the history of the world in that language which you don't understand but which is hers. The stir of the streets perturbs you almost as much as her body, as if the city itself stirred to the rhythm of her cries. Moving, speaking, screaming, running, it flings itself about with laughter, with blows, leaving in sudden bursts, losing itself in the wind coming from the sea. And she is inside you, like the streets, like this city which you are discovering as if better to follow, later, back in the bedroom, the path of her veins, the shape of her sex. She leads you without your really knowing to where, whilst all seems the same, markets, plazas, houses of mud or stone, more plazas, winding streets, market stalls set up at crossroads as if to halt the movement of your bodies.

What is most surprising is the closeness of the animals which mingle with each step you take, with each gesture brought every moment into all these flustered, seriously busy limbs. Everything jumbles together, melting, and the smell of animals surrounds you, mixes with the dust stirred up by men, makes up this vague mixture which troubles you more than anything, more than elsewhere the smells of fuel, the ever-present traces of your world come to invade hers. You no longer know where you are, who you are, what you're seeing. That's not a city. It's nowhere. It's a book you opened as a child, and in which you're losing yourself again, a book which she is writing for you again with the streets, the houses, the faces of her city. You turn its leaves, as just now you leafed through her hair; you slide into it, you stroke these walls as you did that skin which your hand sought beneath the sheets. You follow these streets in amazement as you would a story which isn't yours. But this city is your story, as is this woman in this city. Even the districts ravaged by war are telling you something about your life, your past life of which you fear you'll recoup only ruins, your future life which you no longer know how to construct. You fear seeing your face reflected in the bullet-torn walls, whilst hers is already shining in your memory; you fear drowning in rain-filled craters, you fear wanting to drown there so as not to have to think any longer.

Now your life's appearance has changed, like the war. It's no longer your life, it's no longer really a war. No-one knows what it is.

There's talk of a man who blew himself up not far from here. No-one understands. No-one believes it. There's a feeling however that something is dimly taking shape which they refuse with all their strength to accept but which is stronger than everything, creeping along the streets, oozing from the walls, lifting the roofs. A man who would have chosen death to hasten the end of everything. His head torn off, spat into the skies. His body scattered, his feet tossed into the crowd. Not even from despair. From cold reason. A cold hatred. Against everyone. Against himself. And this city returns to what it never ceased to be, a permanent respite. The only place where you were allowed to experience this final, impossible, unreal love. A love from a book. A love from a play. It needed this setting, soon to be ruined.

You leave this ravaged district and practically run back to the apartment hired for you, paid for you to welcome the reunion of your bodies, chosen by your employer who would never have thought to put you through such a test.

The bedroom is huge; it is empty; naked; lost. Abandoned by her body. You'd think it is just waiting, waiting for that woman to come again to occupy it, to infuse it with her breath, with that scent she gives off, from her limbs, from the joints of her limbs, from her hair which you're still longing to hold in your hands but which is floating about somewhere, far away at the outskirts of her city. You don't know what to do in this great emptiness that she has opened up. You no longer know where to put these arms, these legs which are yours. You want to find something, once again, so as not to keep thinking of her, but everything you see reminds you of her. You can no longer eat without her. You can no longer write or read. You can no longer move. You would like to pick up the phone, have the courage to call those who, cheerfully unconcerned in their innocence which you presume and which you can nevermore share, are waiting for it. But you know if you pick up the receiver the heavy stone will drop onto you again; once again you'll not know who you are, where you are, to whom you're speaking, for whom you're waiting. That's why you're not moving. Doing nothing. Not stretching your arms. You're concentrating on the room's great emptiness; you're trying with all your might to fill it. You're gripping yourself as a while ago you were gripping her hips, her cheeks, her breasts, her thighs. You're trying not to drown. You want to forget those dismal pools amongst the ruins.

When you get up it's to fall to your knees at the foot of your bed.

You'd like to pray. But your God abandoned you days ago. And it's to her God that you speak. In a language you're inventing, a language you're attributing to her, in which your own language is mixed with the words she murmured just now, those words that you're clumsily trying to reproduce. But you mock your own awkwardness, and you mock the ridiculous sight of this man on his knees, incapable of praying, incapable of speaking a comprehensible language. You're mocking him. You'd like to see him weeping. You see him weeping. To you he's even more ridiculous weeping than speaking that pitiful gibberish. A weeping man. A kneeling man. A lone man you're mocking.

But then the telephone rings. It's her, calling you in the middle of the night, that woman who makes that man weep at the foot of his bed. She has left her husband's body, their double bed in that house you don't know and of which she's spoken to you, far from the centre, far from the richness of that centre where mostly people like you come. She hardly speaks. Says two words. Silence. Down the line which joins you there's nothing but the sound of her breathing. Shared silence. Then she says she misses you, she says she's just made love with her husband, that her belly is still wet; she says she didn't cry, that yes, she did cry but it was for you she cried; she says she cried so you could hear her at the other end of the city. She says her husband was happy about it, as you were. You say: As stupidly as me? he liked you crying, thinking it was for pleasure? She says: He gave me pleasure. I cried because he gave me pleasure. Since I met you I think my husband loves me even more, even better, and he really gives me pleasure. As you did.

You say: I'm not your husband.

She says: You're what? What are you to me? Then she goes quiet.

You're hearing words you don't understand.

It's the language of Nur.

Behind her a man speaks her language, that you don't understand.

She hangs up.

You're back on your knees by your telephone, as just now by your bed. You tell yourself you'll perhaps only live like this, on your knees. And then you tell yourself no. You're in a rage against yourself, against your weakness, your cowardice, the miserable distress where you easily wallow, this dribbling self-interest which sickens you. You tell yourself that on the contrary this love will keep you upright for always. That the kneeling is finished, unless by her side. And you get up.

The telephone rings once more. She says it's her again. I can't see you tomorrow. But the day after tomorrow I'll take you far away from here. I want to show you something. I want to show you my country. I send you a kiss. I take you in my arms. I kiss you. My husband wasn't happy. He doesn't know. I'm going back to him. I love him. I love you.

You don't have time to reply, or you don't want to reply; her voice carries you away. She hangs up; she's hung up.

You didn't feel the need to say anything.

You didn't feel the need to ask yourself how you could bear not seeing her tomorrow, nor how to free yourself up the day after to be with her.

You'll see. You know it's not important. You'll find a way. Nothing matters.

And now you don't know how the day after is going.

You don't know what you're doing, what you've done, if you've done it, if you're going to do something. This day after passes as the days of your childhood sometimes passed, in the total absence you inflicted on them. Quite simply, you weren't there. Frankly, this day after passes without you. A rewarding feeling of not existing, of no longer existing. You know, thinking like this, that it's just words; but you know too that there are times when words say something true, when they have the capacity, miraculously, improbably, of not totally being only words.

So that day passed.

Perhaps you walked, crossed streets, plazas, corridors, passed thresholds. Perhaps you did none of all that. You don't know, you've forgotten all about your work. You're already tomorrow. Your body is already over there, ahead of you, to where she's taking you. Your body over there; you here. You, divided. Then you over there, reunited with your body, with her. Reunited over there, all three, you, your body and her. You're already seeing that. You're not seeing yourself walking, passing thresholds, crossing streets, not talking, exchanging, buying selling, paying, selling words, advice, knowledge. You no longer recognise this knowledge that you're presumptuously delivering. You're there without being there, you advance, towards yourself, towards this unfathomable tomorrow that she's promised you.

So that day passed, as if it were written on the list of all the days, that it would disappear without having entirely been.

When you find her again it's as if you'd just hung up the phone, as if her voice had brought you here, to this bus station where she's waiting for you, or rather to this shelter full of holes and ruins, to this crowd jostling you with its morning cries and bustle. And as you take her hand you seem to suddenly find again the contact with her whole body, as if it were all held inside this hand in yours. And you have to take a breath without speaking for a moment, so that you can now launch yourself into this day by her side, climb up into the coach that she's indicating without a word.

Not a coach in fact but a bus. It takes you a long time to understand this strange impression, the strange familiarity of this place she's brought you into. For in this land where you at first feared to come, as one fears a foreign land, instinctively, without being able to do anything about it, the buses are those of your childhood; they are those which ploughed the streets of your own city, thousands of kilometres from here, twenty or thirty years ago, as if time were suddenly flowing back over you, in the form of this bus, an old relic of a bygone world which is ending its life in the streets and on the roads of this country. And at once too you understand what seemed strange to you about them when you saw them running noisily down the long boulevards which surround the city centre and in places cut it in two. Repainted in white on the outside, a white which has become illegible over the years, they have remained the same inside as if to prolong indefinitely their lives as Parisian buses. The same moleskin a thousand times repaired, the same seats facing each other, the same call buttons, cold to the touch but such a silly shape, steel nipples which you and your friends constantly brushed against, laughing, full of adolescent desires. It's as if this woman at your side had just plunged brutally into your childhood.

You would like to explain all that to her, but you don't know how, and you swallow the words which you already feel have no use. And when the vehicle sets off you concentrate on all these passengers who've joined you, often laden with bags which they keep piled up on their knees or heaped in the narrow aisle.

You ask where you're going. She says: to see some stones I love. Some stones, that's all. Is that OK? Near the mountains. We can walk for a bit.

She says nothing more. You don't ask for more. You have no need to know. Getting into this bus—or perhaps it was on taking this woman for the first time in your arms—you'd embarked. You say: we've embarked, and then you laugh, remembering the first time you took her, when she took you. She smiles without understanding what you say. The bus passes the outskirts of the city. The driver has put the radio on, very loudly, a makeshift radio, put together with non-matching speakers, too large for the use being made of them and threatening any unwise skulls which get too close to them. What they hang from is unclear, swaying violently as the bumps increase along the road. You say to yourself that where you live the slightest of these jolts would have the passengers howling; here, each judder makes them laugh. The music spreads among them, twisting between the sounds of the motor and the happy voices of your neighbours. You are amazed at the happiness they all seem to share, as if you alone here could reasonably know it, have the right to it; and you tell yourself straightaway that you will never be rid of your habits of a rich Westerner, convinced despite himself that a certain laugh is forbidden to those who have nothing, or almost. For those here have nothing; you can see from their toothless smiles that physical suffering must be their most ordinary lot, and discomfort, or what you call discomfort, without really knowing what that means. Those bags accompanying them and blocking the exits are perhaps their greatest possessions, cloths from the souks, saucepans bought in the central market, plastic materials exchanged for a few hours' work on building sites. And yet they laugh, more than you could. Together they're singing the words of a song being belted out by the speakers. And all these people united would move you to tears of mixed joy and sorrow if you could at this moment. But you can't, for thanks to this woman at your side you are already far away, lost far away from everything you could have imagined, transported beyond, literally, as if this bus of your childhood had brought you past the impassable limit. Then you listen to them, intently, and you engrave their image deep inside you so as never to forget anything of this moment. Of this music. Of these faces created for all eternity to accompany you on this journey.

The driver who has noticed you begins speaking to you. You don't know how to reply for you don't understand. She translates a few words for you, but not all of it, as if to leave you to find the real questions yourself. You approach the man; you sit next to him, glancing sidelong now and again at the murderous speaker. You try to exchange a few words, with your hands; you repeat words, in your own language and in others you know. He smiles, you smile, he laughs, you do too, and you don't need any more than that. He indicates the road, and something to be seen a long way off; you go along, and suddenly you hear her laughing behind you. She comes up and embraces you, still laughing. Then the driver in his turn bursts out laughing and his laugh seems to bring the whole bus with him. All the voices together, behind your back. All the laughs together, as if now the jolting was nothing but the expression of that profound joy emanating from you and which makes the whole bus vibrate, you who understand nothing and who are happier about that than about any other joy.

The road unwinds before you, scarcely a road, a long ribbon with the asphalt getting scarcer and the ruts more frequent. Along the sides a few carts pulled by bicycles, horses or donkeys are overtaken. The dust stirred up by your passing falls onto them, quickly blown off however by the wind which whistles around the bus's windows. Sometimes old men walking, laden as you would never have imagined possible, without their faces showing any signs of the weight upon their shoulders or their heads; habit removes any trace of a now familiar suffering to the point of affecting even their features. Unless it's simply the joy of living.

Where are all these people going? No houses to receive them, no villages for miles. There are a few buses, crossing or passing you, a few buses like yours or coming from other countries to end their lives in the same way. You'd say the whole world is meeting here, sending the lowest of the dregs of the motoring masses. All sorts of transport, pick-up trucks or 4x4s agleam with grease, all shapes and ages of vehicles, following in line, crossing each other continuously amidst this nowhere where everything converges.

You'd like to question the woman who has come to join you near the driver, learn from her a little more of what you're seeing, but you decide to give in to the fitful jolting which throws you against her and puts an end to any questioning. People talk, shout, dance to the rhythm of the road. And you, lost, are advancing further and further along this path where a friendly hand is leading you. Whilst an hour or more goes by in this wonderful uncertainty, you don't notice the increasing solitude and lack of vehicles.

The first stop is the last. You understand that when you see the bus turning back the way it came, having unloaded its cargo of songs and badly wrapped parcels. But before that you have to say goodbye. With gestures, waving and shaking of hands, finding the piece of paper on which the driver has written his telephone number. He knows as well as you that it won't be possible to call him, that you couldn't talk to each other, just say your given names, his which precedes the six small figures on the paper, yours which he tries painfully to pronounce whilst you repeat the single syllable; he knows all that, but it doesn't matter. This little piece of paper, these clumsy figures, are the sign that you're both alive, that you are the same, that he's a man and you are too, that perhaps he loves two women, like you, that perhaps he has understood you, guessed, and that anyway talking doesn't get you very far.

All the passengers have alighted at the entrance to a non-existent village. Eight, ten houses stuck on this small plot are not enough for all these noisy and jubilant people who say goodbye to you as they leave. They scatter to right and left, without it being obvious where they're going, whether they'll disappear suddenly or slowly melt into the distant hillsides.

You've already given up asking, given up on questions as well as answers. You prefer to imagine that here bodies are lighter, disappearing into the air the further away you get from everything you've left behind. Or that they're going back to the small cemetery up here, on a hill dominated by a mausoleum, a blue dome, dazzling, like a piece of the sky on four walls.

And as she leads you along a path at the side of the road now the houses are disappearing, at the place where the bus left you. Behind you, like another burden you are shedding, it remains alone between heaven and earth. You turn, to see it slowly getting smaller, as if with it you must abandon yet another part of your old life. What? You don't know.

You know nothing.

Once again you know nothing.

You only know your step is lighter as if you'd been living with suffering until now without even noticing it, with a fear until this very point in your life which you will slowly shed as you walk along.

Your feet carry you. You'd say they walk without you. But you know that it's she who makes them move forward. You know it's she who draws you along as if she were calling you from far away.

You tell yourself that you've finally got going, after waiting so long, so long wasting your limited time, that at last you've given up being ready, believing that you had to know where you were going before loading up the animal. You tell yourself that you have at last accepted what happened, that you've not rejected the inexorable, that you've not sought to oppose it with ideas, reasons, knowledge. Or with duties which would protect you by stopping you moving on.

So you move on without shame, treading in this woman's footsteps, without trying to take control, as when you gave yourself up to her arms, to the rhythm of her body. And you see that whatever you do now, she's the one who leads you, straight ahead, amid the stones. You give up trying to understand, to know, to want something other than this presence beside you, before you— inside you. You tell yourself that now the thought will soon arrive, that it will make you weep, weep at not having known before that it was there that you would have to go. Weep for having to come back from there. For you know too that you will have to.

Now all you can do is be carried along the way. What is promised to you, as you know, will await you and nothing will stop you having it, if not you yourself.

So you walk.

You would like to beg for a few words from her, a caress, why not her lips and all that follows. But her gaze is enough, and her gaze doesn't leave you, not even when she isn't looking at you. Better than her hand that you're burning to take, like the one you loved as a child and did not dare to seize.

Besides, are you so different from that child that you still call upon sometimes in the dark, that you called before you found her? Between you and him, the gap hollowed by that old death has closed—as if this woman that you'd like to hold in your arms, in the middle of the path, but whom you stop yourself taking like that so as not to slow down what has started, as if this woman has reconciled with you that part of yourself you thought you'd lost. Beside her you are again that child, not fearful of being him, freely, joyously. Between you and you there is no longer that impassable distance that your life had put there. Between you and you there is this woman. There is this woman who leads you and reunites you. There is this woman. An unknown woman you're discovering with each new step. An almost mute woman who speaks your language with difficulty and who is teaching you to say nothing. And you guess vaguely that if she's brought you here, to this quasi desert, it's to teach you the importance of silence between you, of this silence between her clumsy words and yours. To teach you that and other things you anticipate and allow to come. As if, to arrive at this precise point where she wants to lead you, you needed first to leave everything behind; as if the days beforehand, even with her, even at her side, even in her body, had been nothing more than the beginning of something even more incomprehensible, more impossible, than all you have imagined.

So, you move forward, you follow this woman in the daylight of this incredible country, you follow her without fear, and with joy.

You know already that what she wants to show you is not the most important thing.

The track is no longer a track; the lane is no longer a lane; the path is not even a path. It's her and her alone who seems to be opening the way, between the dry earth and the sand from who knows where, brought by who knows what wind, between the stones and the tufts of grass which perhaps have lived or been dead for thousands of years.

With your European's words you are suddenly thinking stupidly, as if only that would still make you dream, about: lunar landscape; you speak these words in your head and straightaway regret them. Then others arise, prevent you simply looking at what is in front of you. And more arrive to slow you down.

You dismiss the words.

You return to what she's proposing. Your story. Her pictures. You just keep a void around you. You make a void as if it were not complete enough beneath your feet. You surround yourself with it. It protects you. You chase away words so as not to block all the exits.

And you keep going amid dust and sunshine. The sun like that in a book you read long ago, the only one which at this moment you don't reject, a book and a sun leading to a crime; but here the only crime would be to forget this moment, the only death is that of your two bodies, yours and that of this woman you did not know ten days ago. The only event, the event of her presence and yours.

Sometimes you walk with your eyes closed. At the far end of this remote plateau, almost at the edge of a ravine, only her hand guides you. You're playing with her that game with which, long ago, you confronted your own fear. But this time, you're no longer trembling.

Not because she's holding your hand. It's something else making fear impossible. A feeling you weren't aware of, and which perhaps you'll never know again. A certainty.

Sometimes you open your eyes, you see the steep drop beside you; at the bottom, a riverbed and a few branches trying to turn green. You tell yourself all that is yours, and much more than that. She is yours. And you too, at last you are yours.

You feel hot, but you don't know if it's from the endless sun or from this woman, or even from what she's making you confront in yourself. Out of her bag she takes a small plastic bottle; the label, damaged but still stuck to the bottle, as if to defy time passing, carefully re-stuck more than once, this label with its blue letters has a strange effect in this country with its volcano and its green hillsides, with its name from your country but its lettering in her language.

You thank her for having realised you were thirsty. You drink. You give her back the bottle. You watch her lips grasping the bottle's neck in their turn. You'd like to take them in yours once again. You don't do it. You know it's not the moment, the path is calling. You start walking again between the rare grasses until she speaks to you.

She says: See. She doesn't say: Look. Perhaps because she doesn't know the difference. She says: See. You see.

It's bare.

It's alive.

Flat, empty surface. And hills all around.

Nothing hanging there. No flowers. No water. But it's alive. It vibrates. Lines, more lines in the distance, some curved, others broken, others straight, absolutely.

She's walking alongside you, stops; she looks straight ahead; then looks at you looking at that, then looks at you looking at her, with nothing around you both to stop these looks. She closes her eyes. You keep looking at her. Then you close your eyes in your turn. You hear her opening hers and looking at you again. She takes you in her arms; she hugs; she hugs you. Tightly enough to hurt. It hurts. You don't cry. Later, you already know, you'll come back here to cry this cry that you didn't cry. No echoes in the desert. Words leave you, never to return. Nothing returns.

But now she relaxes her hold. You watch her, amazed. You're discovering that impossible sister being given to you here, through that love, which one would say was forbidden, which until now you thought was. That love you desire and which you refuse. You wonder if this woman in the desert is really a woman. You're not sure that she isn't one of those spirits who appear along a road to distract a traveller from his route, for better or worse. You try to remember when she appeared to you for the first time, where. But you can't, and you continue looking at her, unbelieving.

You say: Are you a jinn?

But she doesn't understand. And you realise that here too that word no longer has only one meaning, that the spirits have flown away for ever and that only their trousers remain, so to speak.

Then you laugh; you'd like to remove hers despite the heat and the sun; then she laughs too. But you take her hand and you walk on.

You no longer know very well how long you've been walking like this in silence, amid the rustling of the dry grasses and the spinning stones. Nor do you know how long it is since you left the town, nor even how long since you left your country, those you love, still, more than ever. You're enjoying, genuinely, this moment of absence which you feel will never happen again. You're in the middle of the desert, or it's as if, with this woman. When she stops and says: it's here, you don't react straightaway; you don't even remember that your journey had a purpose; perhaps she told you, perhaps not. You weren't thinking of it.

You look without thinking at what's in front of you.

It's a pile of rocks, rising imperceptibly. At first you see nothing. But as she doesn't move you look more closely, as if to understand what is gripping her and should also catch your eye; she does nothing to help you. You concentrate like a child. You concentrate so hard that finally you make out what gives these rocks their strange appearance, both wild and familiar. It's not their shape which attracts you as you're captivated. It's like a shadow spreading through smudges, through panels, through packets. And suddenly you see patterns engraved there, hundreds, thousands of patterns. Hardly patterns. Black dots, in a row, making body shapes as far as the eye can see, bodies everywhere, on all the front of all the stones into the far distance.

First you see animals, of all sorts, of all sizes, come from long ago, out of what imagination? And you think again of the jinns just now, but this time you don't laugh. They're there, within reach. You could almost feel them. You see them drawing on the stones these thousands of fabled bodies before they retreat into the depths. You don't understand how, in this nowhere she's brought you to, such a crazy population can live. For it does live. It is the stones that live. That move. That run. That creep. Animals with four paws, with six, with eight, some with several heads, several bodies; others which you think you recognise; others which escape at the very moment you'd like to grasp them: horses? bulls? mammals from another age? Each one of them turns his face towards you. Their thousands of eyes are look- ing at you both. They have invaded this corner of the earth, as it they've waited for you for all eternity, you with her, she and you united beneath their peaceful gaze. They've come to wait there; sent by whom?

She's speaking to you, and you understand it wasn't the jinns who did that, but real men. They came to put down here that time immemorial which brought them. They placed it there, right on the rocks, drawing not their feet or their hands as others before and after them had done, but leaving their most intimate traces, their wildest visions. The most joyful too. Their most delicious nightmares. Dreams etched right upon the stones.

You also hear her telling you that the scientists of your own country, or of a country like your own, came to photograph all that, that they said it was extraordinary, how many thousands of years? Then they'd left, gone back home. That no-one ever heard of them again. That perhaps they'll come back. You're telling yourself already that you'd rather they didn't ever come back.

In front of you, they're flowing along all the surfaces, following each other in waves, in leaps, in rebounds. They spread from one block to another. Endlessly flowing and watching you both.

And as you stay motionless before this unbelievable herd, she takes your hand again, forces you to walk on, pulls you towards a taller heap of stones, a more pressing shadow, a wide-open mouth into which you follow her.

Your patient eyes.

Your eyes open to the darkness.

Your eyes which open gradually to the beneficent darkness in the heart of the desert.

But behind you the sun is pushing, pushing you inside. It comes inside with you both, abruptly, whilst flashes of light through the stones open up the view, tiring those eyes which are receiving here more than their due.

She stretches her finger; she points to two holes in the stone, strangely naked, like the impression of two bodies upon the rock, side by side. You could almost detect the shape of a head, the trace of a pelvis.

It's a couch.

A tomb.

Not a tomb. A chamber of death. A chamber of love.

Obstinately, you look at this bed, this chamber.

On the stones around you, still these black dots, tattoos which a madman of long ago came to draw for you, all around and above. These are no longer the fabled animals of outside. These are quite simply bodies. Human bodies. Like you. Like her. Like those who lay here and which you are patiently trying to find. Mingled bodies of men and women. Holding each other, penetrating each other, abandoning each other, returning one to another, leaving each other, drawing together again, penetrating each other again. Heads between legs, fingers in vulvas, penises in mouths, mouths against buttocks, buttocks upon faces. Bodies in love embracing furiously, mountains of loving bodies to accompany death. It is no longer a grotto in the desert; it's a belly, the womb where she had to bring you, where it was written that she, this woman, would bring you before you return to your real life.

You take her in your arms. You think about that nuptial tomb where you would like to lie. You embrace her and you make her slide with you; you no longer know who is trembling, you, her or that skin of a stone upon which you're slowly falling. No carpet, ever, has seemed to you softer than the dust of this tomb, warmer than the cold of this floor.

Then, in this stone chamber, there are cries rising up, cries you recognise. Cries that will haunt you forever, like those of that other chamber far away, in the amazing city. One would say the fabled animals are lowing, coming back to life. Or else the embracing bodies, above your heads. And one no longer knows who is calling, her, the animals or those images looking at you in their obscene postures. And again it's undulating, running over all the surfaces, spreading. Fluid flowing down cheeks, down breasts, down genitals, down limbs entangled, upright, rubbed, bathed in that mud made by your sweat, your saliva, your sperm, mingled with dust. You finish by looking like this grotto. You melt into her, as the cries diminish and the pleasure increases, so much so that even crying becomes impossible. Your breathing becomes more rapid. Your arms keep holding her. You hold her tightly. You hold her. You hear her dying, calling you in the silence of these beginnings, of this end of you, of her—you'd like to say of the world. And whilst you're saying that, those pitiful and ridiculous words, those stupidly grandiloquent words, you start to laugh, as if none of that were serious, in this cave, hollowed out for the gods and for the dead, in the middle of the desert. You laugh at yourself and at those words which pass through you whilst you're doing that, that thing, here, on this dusty floor, with her. You're turning in this cave of your head, whilst your bodies roll beneath the dome, whilst her cries no longer come from her wide-open mouth.

How long without talking, with no longer moving? How long lying here? How long crushing her belly, her breasts, as all your muscles give way? Holding her thighs in your hands whilst no breath leaves her mouth or yours? How long? Wanting it all to start again, to stop?

You're no longer moving, you are dead. You have found the pyramid in which to bury your love forever. The tomb where you can hide with her, inside yourself, the secret chamber where you can cradle your solitude against her body.

It is here you'll stay, even if your body continues elsewhere.

You went back to the city, scarcely knowing how and at what time. You remember a man with a wide smile, his white car doing the journey in reverse, a few words exchanged between her and him, a last look at the blue dome, the first houses of the outskirts, nothing.

Nothing more.

You remember nothing more.

You remember everything, her, nothing, that completeness for ever.

Her body.

You saw each other again several times.

You never spoke again about the stone chamber.

Often you went walking again. Often you walked the streets side by side. You passed through crowds.

One day you even nearly died together. The city wanted to keep you, keep you forever. Joined together.

But you continued walking, whilst fear mounted around you. Perhaps that was what you loved best then. That death should take you. That the violence done to this city you had begun to love more than any other, that that violence should become yours.

That it should strike you.

That it should tear you apart.

That you did not survive it.

That only this woman next to you should survive, as if to retain that love, prevent it ending, finishing forever. That with you dead, she should stay there to keep it, as if suspended, eternal, as far as one can dream such a thing. A love, no, not coming to an end but as if stopped, like time or like life, in that nameless war developing around you.

The sirens and ambulances became more frequent every day. And the city finally gave out a long piercing, continuous, cry, without your knowing whether it was inside or outside you.

When you saw you were seeking those places of death she no longer wished to go out. She wanted to keep you in the bedroom.

And then one night you were able to sleep at her side. All night long. You had not thought it would be possible. You hadn't even dreamt of it, as the days passed that you knew would soon end.

You awoke the next morning next to her.

She was able to give you all those hours. To take them from him she loved, to give them to you. You no longer know how she came, nor what you did; but in the morning she was really there, at your side, with you along her body, stretched out saying nothing, doing nothing, not sure whether you had slept, stayed awake, dreamed, loved.

She gave you that whole night. Offered completely, as for the start of another life, unconditionally.

But it was already over.

Everything had been over for a long time.

At the moment when you met her, at the very instant your eye caught her, it had to be already over. You already held her wholly inside you, and she already held you wholly inside her. Everything that followed was just a repeat of that ending which your bodies simply replayed.

You knew it.
She knew it.
You were forever far from each other.
Snatched apart.
Thrown outside yourselves.
You just had to leave.

You leave.

Once past the electronic gates you look at her looking at you one last time from the window. Neither of you gives a sign. Neither speaks. You watch her. She watches you. You're no longer watching her.

You move towards the counter where the other passengers are already gathering.

You no longer know what you're doing here, whilst she is now separated from you by a thin sheet of glass, through which, perhaps, her eyes follow you.

You look for the nearest seat. You sit. You close your eyes. You hear vague sounds of steps around you, announcements from loudspeakers, voices on phones. Like a cloud of moving and speaking. Floats, ready to vanish whenever you decide. Noisy. But the silence inside you is stronger. Her presence inside you is stronger.

Stronger than everything, stronger than you who are ready to collapse, here in this booking hall, in front of everyone.

And as a blinding light appears behind your eyes, you know, you sense, that everything is going to start. You know it's now that everything is starting, that everything that has finished is starting, and that this time it will never end. Never.

You close your eyes, never to open them again.

You lock yourself for ever in that chamber.

A PARTIAL LIST OF SNUGGLY BOOKS